This book is given with love to...

Written and Illustrated by:
Vince Cleghorne

For Kyle, Rache, Amber-Boo,
and "the Bump."

Love you all lots and lots - V.C.

With a huge thanks to:

Allison Wright, Precy Larkins, and Jess Carrol for their
invaluable advice, critiques, and editing.

Andrew Besarab for additional art and creativity,
and Tracy Baxter for everything else.

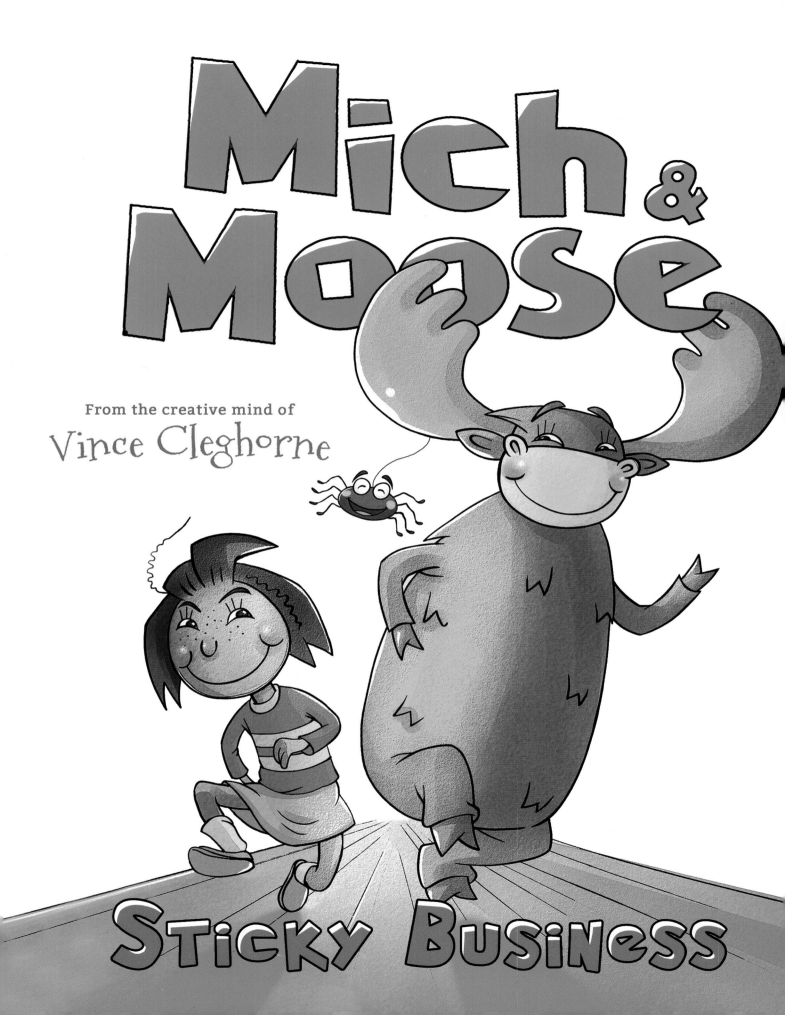

Mich & Moose

From the creative mind of
Vince Cleghorne

Sticky Business

Meet two jolly characters,

Mich & Moose.

They just love snowy mornings...

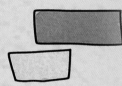

...and this morning was the snowiest!

Mich was the best at throwing snowballs...

Moose made the biggest snow angels...

And together, they built pretty good snowmen.

As the weather grew colder and Moose's teeth began to chatter...

They put on big, woolly scarves and sipped hot cocoa to stay warm.

It was the perfect way to start the day, but not everyone was enjoying the snow.

Spinner the Spider didn't like perfect snowy days, at all!

She had spent her morning trying to stick her web onto a frozen hedge...

A frozen gate...

"I have to find somewhere to stick my web," said Spinner, "or I won't be able to catch any bugs to put in my soup!"

Mich whispered to Moose, "I say we help Spinner! It could be a great adventure."

Moose agreed, "Let's go!"

So Mich and Moose each took a piece of Spinner's web, and set off to find a place where it would stick!

Mich tried a builder's wall,
but it was too drippy.

Moose tried a granny's shawl,
but it was too flippy.

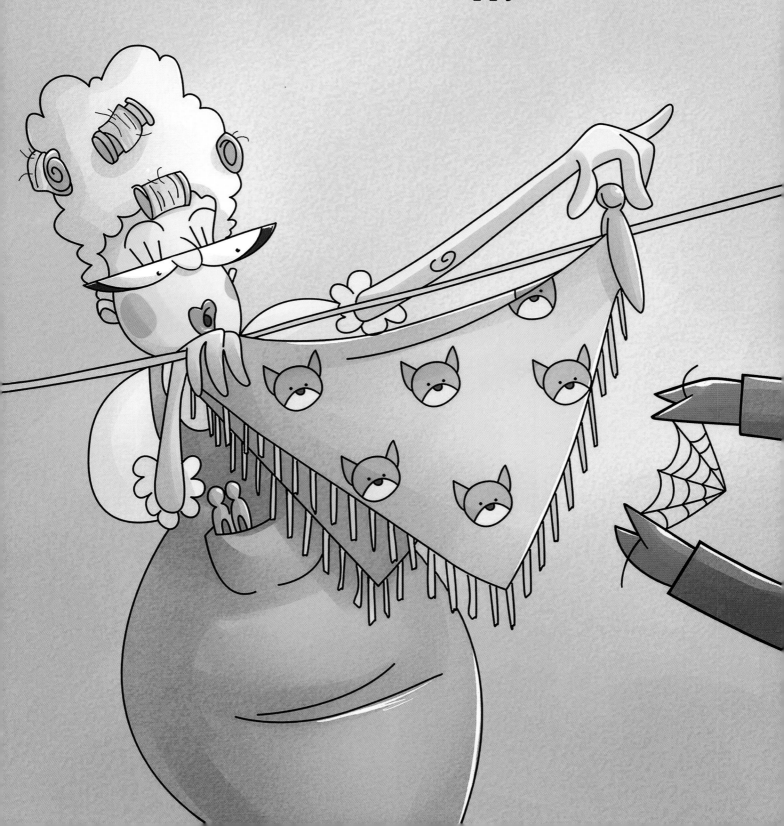

Mich tried a robber's bag,
but he quickly realized.

Moose tried a pirate's flag,
but the ship capsized.

Mich tried a rhino's horn,
but she was busy eating.

Moose tried some sweet popcorn,
but it spilled on the seating.

Mich tried a startled cat,
but it started to yowl.

Moose tried a fancy hat,
but it made the man scowl.

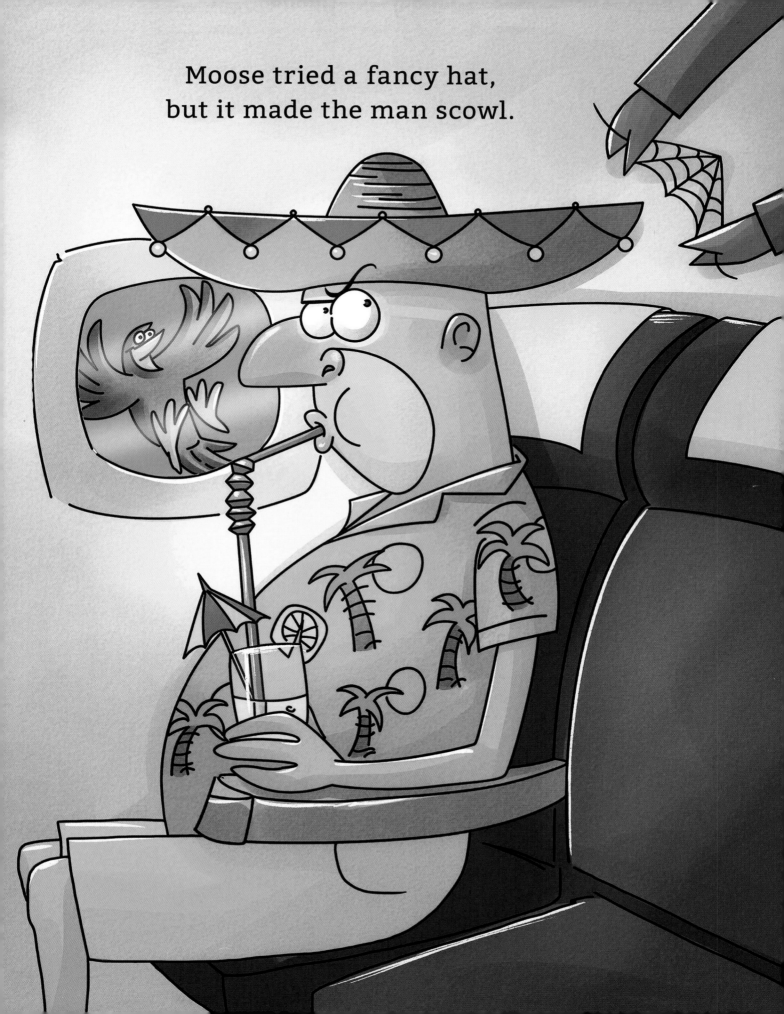

Mich tried a wig in blue,
but it was too floppy.

Moose tried a giant's shoe,
but he was too stroppy.

Mich tried a genie's tum,
but it was jiggly like jelly.

Moose tried a witch's bum,
but it was too smelly.

Then Mich tried a warm doorway,
and the web stuck fast.

Mich and Moose were delighted
and gave each other a high-five!

Then suddenly...

Mich and Moose were sad now,
they hadn't been able to help Spinner.

"We're sorry, Spinner," said Moose.
"But there just isn't anywhere
to stick your web."

Then Mich noticed Moose's shadow
on the snow and began to smile,

"I have an idea!"

With Spinner's web securely stuck
between Moose's giant antlers...

Mich, Moose, and Spinner
sat in the snowy garden
drinking hot cocoa...

Waiting for Spinner to catch the
"ingredients" for her bug soup.

Spinner's soup was full of juicy flies, fat bugs, and crunchy beetles that she'd caught in her lovely new web... Yuck!

We hope you enjoyed the book!

Mich & Moose will be back in a new adventure soon.

Goodbye for now and see you then!

Mich & Moose Activity Sheet

We hope you liked reading the story of Mich & Moose.
Please enjoy the bonus drawing page
we've included for you to add to the story!
Don't forget to include your name and age below
to help remember when you drew this.

Name: _____

Age: _____   Date: _____

Draw Where You'd Stick Spinner's Web

♥ Claim Your FREE Gift!

Visit ➡ PDICBooks.com/michmoose

Thank you for purchasing Mich & Moose, and welcome to the Puppy Dogs & Ice Cream family.

We're certain you're going to love the little gift we've prepared for you at the website above.

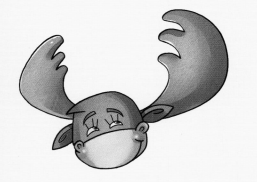